# THE NURSERY VILLAGE

# PUMPKIN · HOUSE

*Peter, Peter, pumpkin eater,*
*Had a wife and couldn't keep her;*
*He put her in a pumpkin shell,*
*And there he kept her very well.*

COLIN AND MOIRA MACLEAN

Kingfisher Books

Peter was the chimney sweep.
  He brushed away the soot,
And went back home to Pumpkin House
  All black from head to foot.

He loved his roly-poly home
  And so did Mrs P.
Just them and Baby by the fire –
  How snug they were, all three.

One morning Peter
went outside.
"What's this?" he yelled.
"Some bumpkin
Has crept around here
in the night
And stolen lumps
of pumpkin."

They patched the holes
and did their best
To keep out wind
and rain...

Next morning even more had gone –
The thief had come again!

The house was cold. The baby woke
And soon began to sneeze.
As Peter went to work he said,
"If this goes on, we'll freeze."

He swept the Porgies' chimney first,
And then who did he spy?

Young Georgie, beaming happily
And gobbling pumpkin pie.

Then Peter went to Muffet Stores
And there who did he see?

Miss Muffet, sipping pumpkin soup
As calmly as could be.

Which child could be the greedy thief?
Poor Peter couldn't tell.
So on he went to Pear Tree Farm
And swept the chimneys well.

His brushes packed, he set off home
As fast as he could go.
But as he ran down Pear Tree Lane
He stopped, and cried, "Oh no!"

He saw two scarecrows in the field;
Their coats were all in shreds.
And there was Mary, putting on
Two brand-new pumpkin heads!

Back home, a loud knock at the door
    Took Peter by surprise.
Outside some village children stood
    In hallowe'en disguise.

With lanterns (pumpkin!) glowing bright
    They sang, then gave a shout:

"We must get home, for after dark
    The Wicked Witch flies out."

"The witch!" cried Peter. "She's the thief!
    Who else would dare to creep
Around the house at dead of night
    When children are asleep?"

In bed both Peter and his wife
   Lay wide awake that night,
As *something* prowled around and kept them
   Shivering with fright.

When morning came, they peered outside
And oh, what a relief!

A *goat* lay snoring on the grass –
   At last they'd caught the thief.

"He's from Shoe Cottage," Peter said.
   They took him straight back home.

"He's eaten up our house," they said.
    "You shouldn't let him roam."

"I'm sorry," the old woman said,
    Then handed them a seed.
"It's magic. Just you watch it grow –
    You'll soon have what you need."

They did...

A giant pumpkin grew
　　(Just like the one before)
And Peter and his family
　　Lived happily once more.

# To Nancy

Kingfisher Books, Grisewood & Dempsey Ltd,
Elsley House, 24–30 Great Titchfield Street,
London W1P 7AD

First published in paperback in 1993 by Kingfisher Books
2 4 6 8 10 9 7 5 3 1
Originally published in hardback in 1992 by Kingfisher Books

BRITISH LIBRARY CATALOGUING IN PUBLICATION DATA
A catalogue record for this book is available
from the British Library

ISBN 1 85697 005 1

Phototypeset by Waveney Typesetters, Norwich
Colour separations by Scantrans Pte Ltd, Singapore
Printed in Spain

*Many of the characters in this book
have appeared in other Nursery Village titles:*
## PEAR TREE FARM
## SHOE COTTAGE
## MUFFET STORES
## THE POST OFFICE
## CASTLE COLE